|| Shri Goverdhandharo Vijayate ||
|| Shri Navneetpriyo Vijayate ||

First published in India by HarperCollins *Publishers* 2025
HarperCollins *Publishers* India, Cyber City,
Building 10-A, Gurugram, Haryana-122002, India
www.harpercollins.co.in

2 4 6 8 10 9 7 5 3 1

Copyright © Goswami Vishal Nathdwara

P-ISBN: 978-93-6989-402-4
E-ISBN: 978-93-7307-068-1

All rights reserved. No part of this publication may be reproduced, stored in a retrieval system, or transmitted, in any form or by any means, electronic, mechanical, photocopying, recording or otherwise, without the prior permission of the publishers.

Without limiting the exclusive rights of any author, contributor or the publisher of this publication, any unauthorized use of this publication to train generative artificial intelligence (AI) technologies is expressly prohibited. HarperCollins also exercise their rights under Article 4(3) of the Digital Single Market Directive 2019/790 and expressly reserve this publication from the text and data-mining exception.

Presented by Dixita Vishal Goswami

Translated by Yatra Shah (Braj Bhasha to English)
Written by Bhavini K. Desai
Illustrated by Meeranjali Bhagwanji
Designed by Radhika Bhagwanji
Legal Support by Dushyant K. Desai

Original Source Material – Shrinathji ki Pragatya Vaarta

www.theadorableshrinathji.com

Printed and bound at Nutech Print Services – India

HarperCollins Publishers, Macken House, 39/40 Mayor Street Upper, Dublin 1, D01 C9W8, Ireland

THE ADORABLE SHRINATHJI

CURATED BY GOSWAMI VISHAL NATHDWARA

HarperCollins *Publishers* India

FOREWORD

Hello,
My name is GVN. Your parents may tell you that I am Vishal Bawa.

Many hundred years ago, my great-great-great-great-greatest grandfather, Shri Vallabh, blessed us with a treasure. A treasure that has united the pious and the faithful across places and time, as well as giving them the joy that only a devotee can experience. I call that treasure Prabhu. You may call it Shrinathji or Shriji or Shriji Bawa. This is the story of his arrival on this Earth and how he regaled and fulfilled the wishes of the faithful with his lilas and his divinity. This is also the story of my most-holy great-great-great-great-greatest grandfather, a sweet little intelligent girl, a white cow and a young boy who grew up to be a poet.

This story will charm you, inspire you and bring you closer to understanding the divinity of Shrinathji. I hope you enjoy it. And I hope you keep them all in your heart.

Happy Reading.

@goswami_vishal_nathdwara

CONTENTS

Chapter 1: Urdhva Bhuja Pragatya
How Shrinathji's Left Hand Appeared

Chapter 2: Shri Mukharvind Pragatya
The Day Shrinathji's Face Appeared

Chapter 3: Dudhpaan
How Shrinathji Drank Milk

Chapter 4: Saddu Pande ko Sakshat Aagya
Command to Saddu Pande

Chapter 5: Saddu Pande ki Gaushala
Saddu Pande's Cowshed

Chapter 6: Dharamdas ko Aagya
How Dharamdas Brought a New Cow to Saddu Pande

Chapter 7: Madhavendra Puri ka Manorath
When Madhavendra Puri served grains to Shrinathji

Chapter 8: Iccha-Purak Shrinathji
Shrinathji Grants Wishes

Chapter 9: Shri Vallabh ko Hukum
How Shrinathji Called Shri Vallabh to Vraj

Chapter 10: Haridasvarya
How Shri Vallabh Came to Vraj

Chapter 11: Pratham Milan
When Shri Vallabh and Shrinathji Met

Chapter 12: Seva Pranali
How Shri Vallabh began Shrinathji's Seva

1
URDHVA BHUJA PRAGATYA
How Shrinathji's Left Hand Appeared

In the land of Vraj, there stood a huge mountain made of dark stones. The stones were so dark, that they almost looked black. Here on this mountain there were peacocks and monkeys, cows and tigers, all living in harmony with each other. This mountain was called Govardhan.

Cowherds and cattle-rearers lived around this mountain. They had hundreds and thousands of cows that gave so much milk each day, enough for a river to flow. The cowherds made a living by churning and selling curd and butter out of the milk.

One day, one of these cowherds lost one of his cows. He waited and waited for her to return, but when she didn't, he started climbing the mountain in search of her.

And what did he see!

A divine left hand, dark in colour, curved up as if lifting something, was peeping out from the top of the Govardhan mountain. Excited by this sight, he ran down and called a few other Vrajvaasis.

'Look what's appeared on Govardhan!'

He showed them. It looked like a miracle, and they all started discussing which *devta* this could be, and where could it have come from. It was the day of *Nag-Panchami*, when the rest of India worshipped the Snake God with milk. So they even considered that.

But among them was a wise old man, who shook his head. 'This must be the *swaroop* of *Shri Krishna*,' he suggested, 'when he had lifted this very Govardhan mountain for seven days with his left hand!' The others listened to him enraptured, as the old man narrated the tale.

'Five thousand years ago, in *Dwapar Yug*, when *Indra Dev* let loose rain and storm on Vraj, a young Krishna had saved the village. He had lifted this mountain on the little finger of his left hand, and all the Vrajvaasis had come and taken shelter under it. After the storm passed, the Vrajvaasis had cheered and worshipped Krishna's left hand. This must be that hand …'

All the villagers stood mesmerised. And believing the wise old man, they too worshipped the curved left hand, which came to be known as *'Urdhva Bhuja'*. While they did this, the old man announced that nobody should try to bring the full deity out.

'It will come in its own time,' he said. 'When the Lord wills it.' The villagers agreed.

As prescribed, they bathed the hand in milk, offered it *akshat*, followed by *chandan*, flowers and *Tulsi* leaves. A feast of rich thick curd and fruits was also offered to *Urdhva Bhuja*. And so, every day they came and worshipped the hand, sometimes bringing fruits and curd, sometimes fresh milk and sweets. And *Urdhva Bhuja* fulfilled their wishes.

Whoever bathed it in milk was granted their heart's desire. It became such a phenomenon that if somebody's cow got lost, they would come to *Urdhva Bhuja* and bathe it in milk. Miraculously, their cow would be found! Someone wanted a child, they got a child. Somebody wanted their cows to give more milk, they gave more milk. And so the miracles of *Urdhva Bhuja* continued.

For 69 long years, nobody tried to pull out the full deity, because the people of Vraj were happy worshipping *Urdhva Bhuja*, the deity's left hand.

2
SHRI MUKHARVIND PRAGATYA
The Day Shrinathji's Face Appeared

It was a warm summer day in the month of *Vaishak*. Sixty-nine years had passed since *Urdhva Bhuja* had appeared. However, on the afternoon of this fine day, the *mukharvind*, the divine beautiful face associated with that left hand, appeared over the rocks of Govardhan. It had big beautiful eyes cast downwards, a strong square jaw, lips like the petals of a lotus and a colour that was as dark as the rain clouds. It was an adorable face.

From this day on, all those friends who had played with Shri Krishna in *Dwapar Yuga* started taking birth in the places around Vraj. It was like a divine theatre, where everything was arranged. And now the show began.

On the night before this divine day, in Champaranya, a South Indian scholar named Laxman Bhatt and his pregnant wife Ellemagaru had stopped on their way south. Ellemagaru was going to give birth to their child. It was earlier than expected, the child had not fully grown in her womb yet. She prayed and prayed to the Lord that the child be born well.

But when the baby boy came out, he was lifeless. He did not cry, did not breathe. Heartbroken, Laxman Bhatt wrapped the small lifeless baby with leaves, and left him under a tree in the jungle.

Later that night, as both were asleep, his wife suddenly woke up from a dream, panting. 'What is it?' Laxman Bhatt asked. 'Our baby, our baby ... he is alive! There is fire around him. He is crying ... alone in the jungle. Let's go and get him, please ... I saw him, please let's go and get him!'

Laxman Bhatt may not have believed her, but his wife was so sad that he took her to the place where he had left their lifeless baby.

And there he was, exactly as she had said! The baby was crying in the cocoon of leaves, sucking his thumb, surrounded by a bright orange fire.

In the dark of the night, they got to their baby who had miraculously been given a new life. They named him Vallabh. And he later came to be known as Shri Vallabhacharyaji; the incarnate of Shri Krishna and his beloved Radha, who had come to serve *Urdhva Bhuja* on Govardhan and teach the world about Shri Krishna and love.

3
DUDHPAAN
How Shrinathji Drank Milk

On the foothills of Govardhan mountain, there was a village named Anyor. Here lived a cowherd named Saddu Pande. He was rich, as he had 1000 cows in his shed. They gave lots of milk every day, and he made lots of butter from it. One of the cows in his cowshed was called Dhumar.

During their grazing time, Dhumar played and ate grass with other cows of Saddu Pande. But moments before sunset, she would leave the herd and wander away, climbing up the Govardhan mountain. This kept going on for more than six months and nobody noticed. Because every day she would come back on time and returned home with the other cows.

One fine day, Saddu Pande noticed that Dhumar's milk production had gone down. He decided to follow her all day and see what she was doing that was affecting her milk output.

She did nothing out of the ordinary, chomping on grass …

Playing with the other cows …

… and enjoying stomping around the foothills of Govardhan. Saddu Pande almost gave up as the time for the cows to come home neared.

But just at the hour of sunset, he saw that she was turning away from all the others and running up towards the mountain. He came out of hiding and quickly followed, leaping and running to keep up with her. She climbed the mountain with great speed and Saddu Pande panted for breath as he kept pace behind, using his hands and feet to grip the rocks while climbing.

Just before the sky turned orange and the sun was about to set, Saddu Pande saw Dhumar stop above the face and left hand of the deity of Govardhan and release her milk. Saddu Pande stood stunned as the adorable divine face opened his mouth and let the milk flow directly in, relishing every drop. Saddu Pande dropped to his knees and bowed down to this incarnate of Shri Krishna, who was hungrily drinking the milk of a cow that came from his cowshed.

4
SADDU PANDE KO SAKSHAT AAGYA
Command to Saddu Pande

Dhumar, the cow, was feeding her milk to the divine face. The white flow looked like nectar, going straight from her udders into his open mouth. As she fed him, Saddu Pande looked on. His heart filled with joy. But then the divine face turned and surprised him by talking directly to him—

'I live on this Govardhan mountain,' the divine face said. 'I am *Devdaman*. My name is also *Indradaman*, because I brought Indra to his knees. When Indra unleashed a storm on Vraj, everyone wanted to run away. But I came and lifted this mountain, made a shelter for my people and foiled all his plans.'

Saddu Pande blinked, his heart racing fast. This was a story that had been associated with this God for so long that he couldn't even remember. But then the divine face added, 'I am also called *Naagdaman*. Because I defeated the evil *Kaliya Naag*. That ten-headed snake was polluting my beloved *Yamuna river*. So one day when we lost our ball in the Yamuna, and none of my friends would go in, I dived in. I fought *Kaliya Naag*, danced on his head. Then sent him packing on his way.'

Saddu Pande was listening intently now, feeling so special that he was getting to hear of such divine *lilas*. From the hero himself!

'Once,' the divine face narrated, 'all my friends were kidnapped by the Creator of the World—Brahma Dev. He didn't believe that I was the master of the Universe. He was trying to test me. So for one earth year, he didn't return my friends to me. But when he peeped into Vraj to see what was happening, he found all my friends playing with me, eating with me, swimming in the Yamuna river … as if they had never disappeared.'

Saddu Pande gasped, his eyes bulging wide. 'I had cloned myself to become many,' the divine face hinted. 'My friends were all me. That is when Brahma Dev brought my friends back, and bowed down to me.' When the divine face stopped talking, Saddu Pande suddenly realised how sweet his voice was. It was like music to his ears. He wanted the music to go on. And the divine face obliged.

'I am the conqueror of eight devtas,' the divine face announced.

'I won over Kuber—the God of Wealth, Chandrama—the God of Darkness, Vaayu—the God of Wind, Varun—the God of Sea, Mrityu—the God of Death, Agni—the God of Fire, Kaamdev—the God of Love, and Shiv—the destroyer. I am that swaroop. That is why my name is *Devdaman*.'

Thus, having narrated the tales of his many names, the divine face affectionately ordered Saddu Pande, 'I always drink the milk of Dhumar. She belongs to the family of cows that lived in my father's cowshed. I still only want to drink her milk. So please feed it to me twice every day.'

Hearing this, Saddu Pande felt blessed. He was so happy that this divine face had spoken to him, told him the stories that only a few elders of Vraj knew. He was even happier that the divine face had asked him to bring milk. So Saddu Pande bowed in front of the divine face and prayed, 'I will do as you say, Lord.'

5
SADDU PANDE KI GAUSHALA
Saddu Pande's Cowshed

Saddu Pande returned home overjoyed that evening, excited to tell his family the tale of the divine face of Govardhan mountain. His house in Anyor was run by his wife Bhavai, along with their young daughter Naro. He gathered them together and announced, 'Today I met the most divine form of God. He resides up on Govardhan, and our Dhumar climbs up every day to feed him her milk.' Bhavai gasped and Naro grinned, excited at the prospect of such an interesting story.

'He asked me to bring Dhumar's milk every morning and evening to him ...' Saddu Pande remarked. 'He spoke to you? Really, Baba?' Naro asked, even more excited than she was before.

'Yes! Yes, Naro! He speaks. This God speaks; and what a beautiful voice he has. He is the Krishna of our Vraj, who lifted Govardhan and defeated Indradev ... What fortune have we been blessed with that Lord Krishna asks us for milk! Bhavai, make sure you don't milk Dhumar for our usual stock. Instead, Naro will take her milk up to the divine face on the mountain. Every morning and evening without fail.'

And so began a new routine ritual in Saddu Pande's home. Naro would milk Dhumar twice a day, collect her milk in a big bowl, and climb up the mountain to feed the divine face. On days she got late, the face would call out in his rich and sweet voice, 'Naro, O Naro …' beckoning her. This went on for a long time, the divine face happy to be fed, and Saddu Pande's family happier to feed.

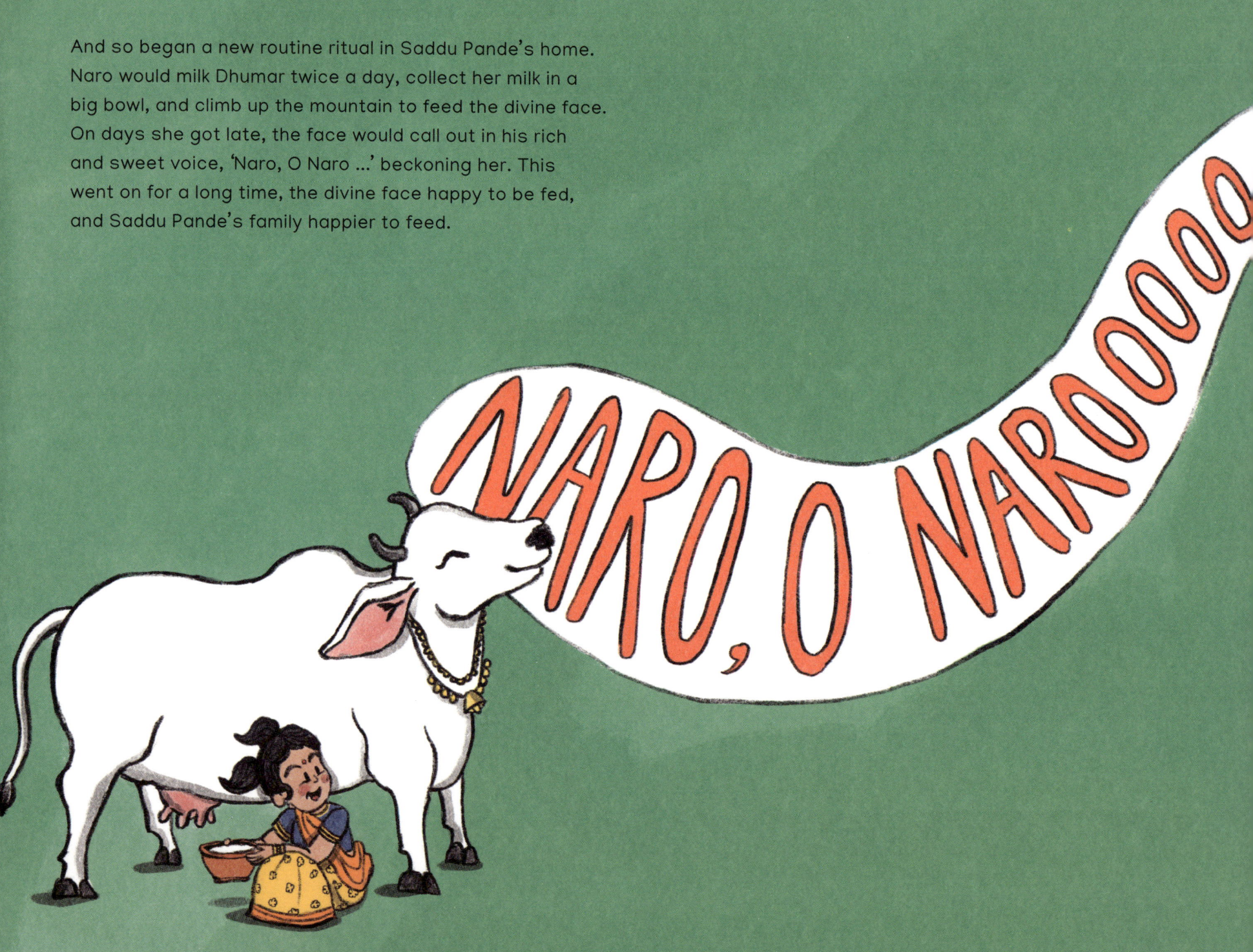

Then one day, Dhumar stopped giving milk. Saddu Pande was devastated. He didn't know what to do. It was time to feed the divine face and his cow's udders had dried up. So he filled the bowl with the milk of another cow and sent Naro up, praying that the divine face would accept it. But Naro returned with the bowl still full.

'What happened, Naro?'

'He didn't drink this milk, Baba. He says that he only drinks the milk of Nand baba's cows. I prayed to him, requested him, asked him what should we do. And he announced that tomorrow one cow with ancestry from Nand baba's cowshed would arrive outside our house.'

'But how? Who would have such a cow? And even if they had it, why would they give it to us?' 'I don't know, Baba,' Naro shrugged. 'But if he has said it, it will happen.'

6
DHARAMDAS KO AAGYA
How Dharamdas Brought a New Cow to Saddu Pande

In Vraj, there was a small village called Jamnavati. Here lived a cowherd named Dharamdas. He was a devotee of Chaturnaag and had a nephew called Kumbhandas.

Dharamdas had a huge cowshed, with more than 400 cows. One of them belonged to the family of cows from Nand baba's house. One day, this cow broke away from her herd and wandered up the Govardhan mountain. She released her milk on the divine face and fed him until he was full. Then she sat by his side and did not return home.

Worried, Dharamdas took his nephew Kumbhandas and together they climbed up the mountain in search of their cow. When they found her resting near the divine face and tried to take her back, she resisted and did not move from her place. That is when the divine face spoke again, mesmerising the duo with his deep, commanding voice.

'O Dharamdas, leave this cow to Saddu Pande. I will drink her milk every day. She is the direct descendent of the cow from my father, Nand baba's cowshed. I will only drink her milk.'

Startled, Dharamdas looked at the beautiful divine face, and dropped to his knees. But the divine face wasn't done yet. He turned to the 10-year-old Kumbhandas, and smiled.

'Kumbhandas, you come and play with me every day from tomorrow.'

Enchanted by the nectar and joy in that voice, both uncle and nephew lost consciousness. They fainted right there, falling on their backs. When they regained their senses, they realised that they had actually been spoken to by the God of Govardhan! Overjoyed, they got to their feet and did a *parikrama* of the divine face. Then they did *sashtang dandvat* in front of the deity, by stretching out on their stomachs and folding their hands in front of their heads.

This was a miracle, a deity that asked for milk and called Kumbhandas to play with him. So in accordance with his command, Dharamdas left his cow outside Saddu Pande's house in Anyor and Kumbhandas went to play with the divine face every day.

7
MADHAVENDRA PURI KA MANORATH
When Madhavendra Puri served Grains to Shrinathji

Days passed, seasons changed and the divine face on Govardhan continued to enjoy the love and attention of the Vrajvaasis. He would get milk from his favourite cow, and Naro would carry it up for him to drink. Kumbhandas would come every day to play with him. More of his friends from the time of his Krishna avatar were slowly and steadily taking birth again around Govardhan.

Then one day, a man named Madhavendra Puri came to Vraj. He had come for *Govardhan parikrama* and lived on a raised platform outside Saddu Pande's house. He was a *Gaudiya Vaishnav*, belonging to the Krishna-worshipping sect from West Bengal. And like all other Vrajvaasis, he too was enchanted by the divine face.

Madhavendra Puri would go for his *darshan* every day, and would spend hours just being mesmerised by the sight. He fell so in love with the divine face that one day he picked flowers and made a garland for him. He searched for peacock feathers and wove them together to make a crown. Then a desire sparked in his heart. A desire to feed cooked grains to this deity.

'If only I could ready a meal and offer him ... I could then be blessed with his *prasad*,' Madhavendra Puri thought to himself.

So he cooked some grains, prepared a platter of offering and climbed up the mountain with the adornments he had made. When he reached the divine face and offered the grains, the deity of Govardhan gently turned him down.

'I will partake of grains only when they are fed to me by Shri Vallabh,' the divine face asserted. 'He will come here and cook for me. Until that time, I will only have milk. But Madhavendra Puri, since you have wished to do my *shringar* and cook my *bhog*, I promise you that you will be granted that *seva*. Just not yet.'

Madhavendra Puri folded his hands and bowed his head, 'What is your command for me, Lord?'

'Go and do a parikrama of the country,' the divine face commanded. 'By the time you return, Shri Vallabh will be here. He will have established my throne and built a temple by then. He will employ you in my *seva*. But until that time comes, I am happy to play with my friends and enjoy my *lila* with these Vrajvaasis.'

With this command of the Lord, Madhavendra Puri left for his *Bharat parikrama*, ready to wait for his time. The divine face continued to perform his *lilas*, accepted milk and curd from Vrajvaasis, played with Kumbhandas, stole butter from the villagers' houses and made the wishes of every devotee come true.

8
ICCHA-PURAK SHRINATHJI
Shrinathji Grants Wishes

As the divine face played in the forests of Vraj and stole butter from Vrajvaasis, he also granted their wishes. Whenever a Vrajvaasi faced a problem, they would come to the divine face with their woes. They would pray to him and take a *manyata* of milk or curd offerings. And miraculously, their problem would be solved.

Once, a Vrajvaasi from a place called Puchri came to the divine face. 'My son isn't getting married, Lord,' he prayed. 'If by your grace he gets married, I will offer you 50 kilograms of milk and curd.'

A short while later, his son found a beautiful life partner and got married. The man returned to the divine face, overjoyed and brought pots and pots of milk and curd with him. That incident became a turning point. Not only from Vraj, but also from villages near and far, people started coming to the divine face with their woes. The divine face granted their wishes and accepted their generous offerings.

The miraculous tales of the divine face spread from village to village. A Vrajvaasi from Bhavanpura lost his cow in the forest. He was devastated because the cow was wandering alone in a forest where a lion lived. It was said that no herbivore came out alive from there.

'Please save my cow from the lion, Lord. If my cow returns home safe to me, I will always offer all her milk to you,' the Vrajvaasi prayed.

RRROOAAR!

That evening, as the cow was lost in the jungle, she came face to face with the big, fierce lion. But before the lion could pounce on her, a long arm extended from the Govardhan mountain and pulled the cow by her ear, guiding her out of the jungle.

When the Vrajvaasi woke up the next morning, his cow was sitting in her usual place in the cowshed. Unable to believe the great miracle in front of his eyes, the Vrajvaasi remembered his *manyata* to the divine face and from that day onwards, offered all the milk of that cow to him every day.

On the other side, on the Govardhan mountain, the divine face turned to Kumbhandas and sweetly whined, 'My arm hurts from dragging that cow all the way to her home ... Kumbhna, massage my arm, please!'

9
SHRI VALLABH KO HUKUM
How Shrinathji Called Shri Vallabh to Vraj

Vallabh, the baby that was born in Champaranya on the same day that Shrinathji's divine face appeared on Govardhan mountain, had now grown up to be a young and intelligent scholar. He was touted as learned as well as pious. He had won several religious debates in the South, as well as defeated great thinkers from North India.

A scholar of *Ved, Puran, Shrimad Bhagwad* and other scriptures, he was also a great writer. He was just starting his philosophical journey across India, when a dream-like revelation changed everything for him.

It was a cool, spring day in Jharkhand when a voice came to him. It was such a rich and sweet voice that it sounded like music.

'I have appeared on the mountain of Govardhan as *Govardhannathji*,' the voice commanded. 'The Vrajvaasis have seen my face and they wish to see all of me. But I will not come out. I will wait for you. So come find me as soon as you can. Do my seva and teach my seva to the others. The *jeevs* from my Krishna avatar are all here and waiting for you to guide them.'

Shri Vallabh felt like his life had found its meaning. This command came to him like the calling of everything he was meant to be.

'Come to me,' the voice said. 'We will meet at a place called Haridasvarya.'

10
HARIDASVARYA
How Shri Vallabh Came to Vraj

When Shrinathji asked Shri Vallabh to meet him at a place called Haridasvarya, Shri Vallabh didn't know where to go. So he started north from Jharkhand, and reached the city of Mathura. The tales and *lilas* of Shri Krishna embraced him as soon as he stepped in the land of Vraj. The dust, the water, the air itself was heavy with the essence of Shri Krishna.

Seeking the Lord who had beckoned him, Shri Vallabh travelled further. And soon, he reached the Govardhan mountain, which was so huge that its shadow fell on the Yamuna river. The mountain looked like a giant God itself, made of dark stones, with numerous forests and foothills, animals and birds. Govardhan was flourishing.

Shri Vallabh made a stop at Anyor, at the foothills of the Govardhan mountain, and chose to reside on the same raised platform outside Saddu Pande's house where Madhavendra Puri had stayed. The news of his arrival spread like wildfire throughout Vraj and soon, Vrajvaasis started flocking to see him. They had heard that he was a very gifted young *Aacharya*. But his sight filled their hearts with unconfined joy. They realised that not only was he special, but he was also one in a million, because his face reminded them of the divine face on their mountain.

Foremost among them was Saddu Pande, who came to Shri Vallabh and bowed down to him with folded hands. '*Aacharyacharan*, please come and grace my home with your holy presence. Give us the fortune of hosting you in our humble home,' he prayed.
'I request you to have dinner with us.'

One of Shri Vallabh's disciples, Krishnadas Meghan, came forward. He folded his hands and answered, 'We are very grateful, and happy to accept your hospitality. But *Aacharyacharan* only eats the food cooked by his disciples.'

Before Saddu Pande could speak any further, they heard a deep commanding voice coming from the top of Govardhan.

'Arey Naro, get me my milk!' To which, Naro called back, 'Today we have guests ...' The voice replied, 'I'm happy to hear that you have guests. But get me my milk.'

'Okay! I'll be right up.'

Naro excused herself from the crowd, filled a big bowl with the milk from the divine face's favourite cow, and set off to feed him. That is when Shri Vallabh turned to his other disciple Damla, and asked, 'Did you hear those words Damla?' 'I heard, but did not understand,' Damla replied humbly.

'This is the same voice that had ordered me to come to Haridasvarya!' Shri Vallabh exclaimed. '*Govardhannathji* is right here, up on this mountain. This is Haridasvarya, isn't it?' 'Yes, *Aacharyacharan*,' Saddu Pande agreed and began telling him how the divine face had appeared on the Govardhan mountain.

In no time, Naro was seen skipping back down with an empty bowl in hand. She came to a stop when she saw that Shri Vallabh was waiting for her. 'Is there any milk left?' he asked. 'Yes, *Aacharyacharan*. We have lots of milk in the house,' Naro replied. 'No, I meant in that bowl,' Shri Vallabh pointed to her hand, 'is there any milk left in that bowl?'

Naro looked from the young Aacharya to the empty bowl in her hand. It was swiped clean, as always. The divine face would delightfully drink the milk of his favourite cow. He would never leave any. It was no different today, except for a few drops. 'There is a little ... but I can get you more from the house!' she remarked. 'No,' Shri Vallabh replied. 'I want the milk leftover from what he had. This will be plenty.'

And so, for the first time, Shri Vallabh drank the *Prasadi* milk of Shrinathji, from the same bowl that he had used.

Later in the day, Saddu Pande surrendered himself to Shri Vallabh, and asked him to take him as a disciple. Kind as ever, Shri Vallabh accepted him, gave him initiation through a *mantra* and ate the food that he prepared.

At night, as the moon rose and crickets croaked, Shri Vallabh sat with his disciples Damla, Krishnadas Meghan, Manikchand, Saddu Pande and the other Vrajvaasis surrounding him. 'Please tell me the tale of how *Govardhannathji* appeared on Govardhan,' Shri Vallabh asked Saddu Pande.

Saddu Pande humbly bowed his head and folded his hands. 'You know it all, *Aacharyacharan*. Who am I to tell you a tale that is already known to you?' 'Even so, tell me again.'

On the second command, Saddu Pande launched into the grand tale, narrating how one day *Urdhva Bhuja*—the divine left hand—had appeared on Govardhan, how the Vrajvaasis had thought it was the Snake God, how later the divine face had appeared and started talking, drinking milk and fulfilling wishes. Saddu Pande's narration touched Shri Vallabh's soul, filled his heart with a joy he hadn't experienced anywhere.

'I will climb up to him tomorrow morning,' he decided.

11
PRATHAM MILAN
When Shri Vallabh and Shrinathji Met

The next morning, at the crack of dawn, Shri Vallabh set off from Saddu Pande's house to climb the Govardhan mountain. His disciples and Vrajvaasis followed him.

When he was still some distance away from the peak, the divine face, impatient with excitement, climbed out from within the rocks and started running down towards Shri Vallabh.

It was a sight for sore eyes, as the Vrajvaasis saw the divine deity of Shrinathji for the first time and found him running right into the open arms of Shri Vallabh.

The two embraced as if they had known each other forever and had been separated for ages. Their embrace was full of love and affection.

Their meeting looked like a beautiful painting of contrasts. While Shri Vallabh was fair and wore a white *dhoti* and *upvastra*, Shrinathji was dark as a rain cloud. Where Shri Vallabh was lean, Shrinathji was healthily built. But both their faces reflected each other.

The moment was indescribable! The true beauty of it was only captured when Shri Gopaldasji made a *kirtan* out of it.

12
SEVA PRANALI
How Shri Vallabh began Shrinathji's Seva

Over the next few weeks, Shri Vallabh started arranging for everything that Shrinathji would require. In fact, Shrinathji himself guided him.

'Make me a throne to reside on,' he commanded. 'Make a temple for this throne. Make my *seva pranali* and take jeevs in your shelter. Without these, *seva* will not be accepted in *Pushti Marg*.' As per his wishes, Shri Vallabh made a small makeshift temple, arranged for a throne and had Shrinathji grace it.

He methodically created a simple but firm *seva pranali*, which consisted of a set order and methods of serving the Lord.

From food to garments, decorations to *darshan*, Shri Vallabh designed it all keeping the comfort and contentment of Shrinathji in mind. Then one day, he went down Govardhan mountain in search of someone who could carry out Shrinathji's *seva* just as he had designed it to be.

In a cave near Apsara Kund lived a pious man called Ramdas. He had come across Shri Vallabh and had become his disciple. Now Shri Vallabh asked him to serve Shrinathji.

'But how can I do seva, *Aacharyacharan*? I have never done it before … what if I make a mistake?' Ramdas exclaimed. 'Do not worry Ramdas. Shrinathji will himself teach you what you don't know. And I will show you what I know.'

With that, Shri Vallabh wove a crown out of peacock feathers, gathered beads to make *gunja mala* and taught Ramdas how to do seva.

'Ramdas, every morning, take a bath at Govind Kund before coming up to the temple. Bring a pot of water along to bathe Shrinathji. Once you have bathed Shrinathji, very gently, with great care, use a soft washcloth to pat him dry. Then, adorn him with this gunja mala and adorn his head with this peacock crown,' Shri Vallabh guided.

Ramdas listened with rapt attention.

'Prepare different meals for Shrinathji as he commands. Don't worry, he will guide you daily as to what he wishes to have. Curd and milk are already brought to him by Vrajvaasis, so let them serve him those.'

After prescribing the *seva pranali* in detail to Ramdas, Shri Vallabh turned to Saddu Pande, who was waiting with all the Vrajvaasis. 'I am leaving my everything behind with you, serve him like he is your everything,' Shri Vallabh told them. 'In case Vraj is under attack at any point of time, or any danger looms over Govardhan, then protect Shrinathji first.'

With folded hands, the Vrajvaasis treasured and accepted his word.

That day, Shri Vallabh made a meal of cooked grains for Shrinathji. And for the first time since the appearance of *Urdhva Bhuja*, this deity of Govardhan, this *Devdaman*, this adorable divine face, this Shrinathji, ate a morsel of rice. Shri Vallabh fed him with his own hands, and having ensured that his *seva* would be done rightly and with love, was compelled to set off on his Bharat parikrama.

On this *parikrama*, he would meet beings that would need upliftment, he would take disciples, spread the message of Shrinathji; on this parikrama he would establish *Pushti Marg*—the Path of Grace. The path that would guide the pious beings that had been lost for ages from Shri Krishna, back to him.

While Shri Vallabh would be on his *parikrama*, Shrinathji would take full advantage and create ruckus in Vraj. He would enjoy the *seva* of Vrajvaasis and also loot their butter, he would play with Kumbhandas and also listen to him make poems about their mischief. He would prank his friends and playfully trouble them. He would grant wishes and also become the God of love.

But most of all, he would be adored by one and all, just as he had been in his Krishna avatar.

AFTERWORD

Hello,
I am Dixita Bahuji, the wife of Vishal Bawa. I have two little kids just like you. They keep reading this book over and over again. But let me tell you a secret—they see the pictures more and read less. So you can too.

If you fell in love with the adorable Shrinathji like I did, then ask your parents to tell you more about him. Ask as many questions as you like. That's the best part—the more you ask, the more you will know.

And also, there is more to this story. I will tell you soon.

Until then,
Sweet Dreams.

@dixitavgoswami

COME SEE ME IN NATHDWARA!

GLOSSARY

Aacharya/Aacharyacharan: Teacher

Akshat: Raw rice grains

Bharat Parikrama: A spiritual journey across the Indian subcontinent

Bhog: Food offerings to God

Chandan: Sandalwood

Darshan: An opportunity to view and glimpse the image of a God/deity

Devta: Demigod

Dhoti: A cotton garment for men, tied to cover the lower half of the body

Dwapar Yug: One of the four epochs of the world's time cycle. In Hinduism, time is cyclical, and runs in these epochs—Sat Yug, Treta Yug, Dwapar Yug and Kali Yug. Sinners and evildoers increase exponentially with each Yug until everything is destroyed and restarts again

Gaudiya Vaishnav: A sect of Vishnu-worshipping people

Govardhan Parikrama: Walking around the Govardhan mountain to experience the land of Shri Krishna's lilas

Govind Kund: The Govind Pond

Gunja Mala: A simple necklace made from charnoti plant seeds

Indra Dev: The Demigod of Rain

Jeevs: Souls

Kaliya Naag: The evil dark snake who polluted the River Yamuna. Lord Krishna dived in and fought the snake, defeated him and sent him away

Kirtan: The songs of Shri Krishna's lilas that are sung during seva

Lilas: Divine pastimes and activities like playing, dancing, hanging out with friends … things that Shri Krishna did with Vrajvaasis

Mantra: Divine slogans

Manyata: A divine wish, which if fulfilled, compels you to complete your end of the prayer

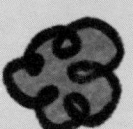
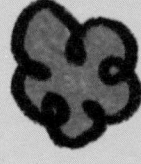

Mathura: The holy town in North India where Shri Krishna was born

Mukharvind: The divine face of Shrinathji

Nag-Panchami: The festival of the Snake God

Parikrama: Walking around a deity/figure in a clockwise circle

Prasad: The sacred food that once tasted by the deity, is offered to the devotees

Pushti Marg: The Path of Grace, where service to Lord Shrinathji is our greatest purpose and source of joy

Sashtang Dandvat: A respectful greeting to a God or teacher by lying facedown on the ground and joining both hands in front of your head

Seva: The daily worshipping and service of Shrinathji

Seva Pranali: The step-by-step process and methods of performing seva and serving the Lord

Shringar: Adornments like clothes, jewellery and flower garlands

Shri Krishna: The Indian God who is dark-skinned, loves to herd his cows, play his flute, and steal butter from his neighbours

Shri Vallabhacharyaji: The Indian saint and scholar who brought the idol of Shrinathji from Govardhan and established Pushti Marg

Swaroop: Idol

Tulsi: Holy Basil plant

Upvastra: A cotton garment for men, worn to cover the upper half of the body

Urdhva Bhuja: The Left Hand of Shrinathji

Vaishak: A month occurring in the Hindu calendar (falls somewhere in March–April)

Ved, Puran, Shrimad Bhagwad: The ancient divine texts of Hinduism

Vrajvaasis: The residents of Vraj

Yamuna River: A North Indian river that flows through Vraj. She is one of Shri Krishna's beloveds too

Visit for more surprises
www.theadorableshrinathji.com